This book belongs to

..................................................

..................................................

..................................................

First published 2021 by Johnny Magory Business. Ballynafagh, Prosperous, Naas, Co. Kildare, Ireland.

ISBN: 978-1-8382152-5-5
Text, Illustrations, Design © 2021 Emma-Jane Leeson
www.JohnnyMagory.com

This book was produced entirely in Ireland (and we're really proud about that!)
Written by Emma-Jane Leeson, Kildare
Edited by Aoife Barrett, Dublin
Illustrated and Designed by Kim Shaw, Kilkenny
Printed on 100% biodegradable and FSC certified paper by KPS Colour Print, Mayo
The right of Emma-Jane Leeson to be identified as the Author of the work has been asserted by her in accordance to Copyright Acts.

Proud Partners of Children's Health Foundation Crumlin.
2% of the proceeds from the sale of this book will be donated to this charity.
Please visit www.CMRF.org for more information.

# Johnny Magory

## Oíche Nollag Adventure

For
Davey, Tina & Amanda,
the Christmas Professionals

Misneach & Brod

Can you name Johnny Magory's friends?
You can learn all about us on his free
Irish Wildlife Directory at
www.JohnnyMagory.com/Animals

Giorria

Gráinneog

Frog

Spadalach

Feadóg bhuí

Luch fheir

Fia buí

Dallog fhraoigh

#JohnnyMagory

Why not have your own adventure and visit
the Phoenix Park in Dublin, Ireland?
It's the largest city park in Europe occupying
7 square kilometres and is home to the
President of Ireland and Dublin Zoo.
There are thousands of species of wildlife
within the park which is bursting with Irish
heritage and history so pack a picnic and
make a day of it!

I'll tell you a story about Johnny Magory,
His sister Lily-May and their trusty dog Ruairi.
These clever two are three and seven years old,
They're usually good
but they're

sometimes

bold!

One of their **favourite** times of year

Is when **Santy** comes with all his reindeer

**AN NOLLAIG** brings **joy** to dark winter nights

And trees full of **baubles** and twinkling lights.

Christmas Eve is magic, the most *fun*,

Johnny **loves** helping to get everything done.

Visiting his cousins
and swapping
**presents** with a grin,

And getting Santy and Rudolph's **treats**
from the special tin.

They leave Santy out a **yummy** mince pie,

And a sup of PORTER to help him to *fly!*

A pot of **hot tea** to keep him warm,

And **carrots** for Rudolph to help him perform.

They watch the RTÉ Nuacht weather report,

And see **Santy** is being helped by the airport.

NUACHT · RTÉ

BREAKING NEWS: SANTA LEAVES NORTH POLE

They brush their teeth and Mammy reads the Christmas book.
Johnny peeps out through the curtains to have a quick **look**.

Their parents tell them,

"Stay in bed until it's Christmas Day,
We know you're excited but that's the Santy rule,"

they say.

The snow falls heavily as they close their sleepy eyes,

"I wish it was Christmas morning already," Johnny sighs.

"Will Santy bring us a **surprise** present?"

Lily-May squeaks.

"If you sleep, mo stór," Mammy smiles, kissing her cheeks.

A few hours later Lily-May awakes to the sound of a bell.

"Wake up, Johnny," she whispers, "Ruairi hears it as well!"

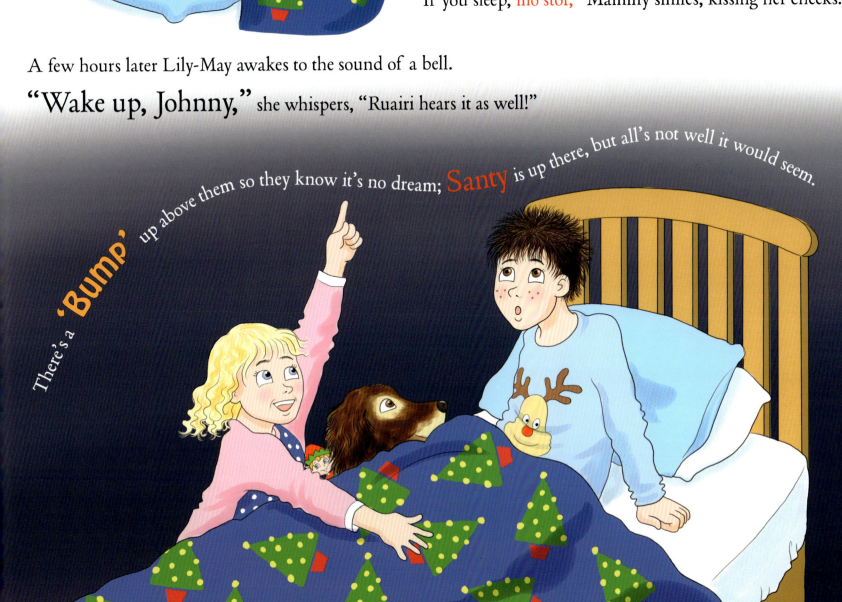

There's a 'Bump' up above them so they know it's no dream; Santy is up there, but all's not well it would seem.

They hear woeful **sneezing** coming from the roof, And one of the reindeer keeps **banging** his hoof.

They get out of bed and tiptoe slowly downstairs;
In the kitchen they see Santy on one of the chairs!

Santy smiles and Ruairi runs in to give him a big lick.

The children launch a loving **hug** upon him

and ask who's sick.

"Donner bhocht," he says,

"my trusty old reindeer,
Is suffering from the flu
caused by the cold air."

"I'm worried, I've **SO MANY** presents to deliver,"

Santy groans, as his lip begins to quiver.

"I know!"

smiles Lily-May
with the **biggest** ever grin.

"I'll ask *Lord Stag* to help you out,
come on, let's find him."

They grab their wellies and take Santy by the hand, **Bursting** out the back door with a torch and a plan.

They run into the Phoenix Park where all the Dublin deer stay,

With the President and the zoo animals so they can all play.

They spot Mr Badger wading through the snow,
They explain their plan and he tells them where to go:

"Around the **oak** at the **Furry Glen Pond** and by the President's dogs,
Don't wake the *wood mice* sleeping inside the old oak logs.
Swing a left before the **Shovelers** and straight down by **Finn Hare**,
Tiptoe by the **Golden Plover's** nest and then you're **nearly there**.

**JUMP** the ditch then slide down the hill straight by *Mr Frog*,
Pass the PYGMY SHREWS at the Hawthorn tree and by the sleeping **Hedgehog**,
In front of her bed you'll see a well-trodden **path** that goes in a zig-zag,
Follow that, my dear friends, and you'll surely find *Lord Stag*."

They hug Mr Badger and say

"Go raibh mile maith agat!"

Then *as quick as they can* their mission begins on foot.

Around the **oak** at the **Furry Glen Pond** and by the President's dogs,

Tip-toeing by the Wood mice sleeping inside the old oak logs.

Swinging a left before the **Shovelers** and straight down by **Finn Hare**,
Creeping by the **Golden Plover's** nest -

"Come on guys, we're nearly there!"

They **jump** the ditch and slide down the hill right past **Mr Frog**,

Then pass the PYGMY SHREWS at the Hawthorn tree and **Mrs Hedgehog**,

They run down the well-trodden **path** that goes in a zig-zag,

Then sure enough, as Mr Badger said, they finally see *Lord Stag*."

Lord Stag is in a peaceful sleep with his BABY FAWN.

He wakes and stares at the trio with a sleepy **yawn**.

Santy explains,

"I need you to replace poor Donner."

Lord Stag agrees with a smile,

"It would be my honour."

"Hooray!"

Santy shouts.
"now we really need to get back.

I've a **country load** of presents
to deliver from my sack!"

He sprinkles **magic dust** on
Lord Stag and Ruairi so they can fly.

The trio jump up on their backs and *zip* across the sky.

Donner's **thrilled** to see Lord Stag has come to take his place.

Santy sends him back to the North Pole's reindeer recovery space.

Johnny and Lily-May don't remember going back to bed.
They wake up and think it was a **dream** about Donner and the sled.

But then they pull off the blankets and notice their mucky wellies,
Still on their feet (AND ON THE LOVELY CLEAN SHEETS!) - and they **laugh** from their bellies!

The children burst down to their parents, shouting

"Nollaig Shona Duit!"

They're full of **CHRISTMAS** spirit,
opening presents without a glitch.

Lily-May spots Lord Stag waiting for her at the windowsill,
They run outside and she snuggles him, saying

## "You're brill!"

Lord Stag has a **special message** for young Lily-May,

"Santy says **thank you**, your quick
thinking saved Christmas Day!"

Lily-May nearly bursts with pride and beams as it begins to snow.

"We'll never forget last night no matter how big we grow!"

She grabs Johnny's hand, as Ruairi's big tail wags, and instead of snow angels, they make snow **stags!**